THIS BOOK BELONGS TO Rob Hook

BANTAM BOOKS
NEW YORK · TORONTO · LONDON · SYDNEY · AUCKLAND

Jim Davis

U.S. ACRES

THE BIG CAMP-OUT

from the creator of GARFIELD®

Written by Jim Kraft
Designed and Illustrated by
Betsy Brackett, Larry Fentz, Dwight Ferris,
Dan Haskett and Brett Koth

Booker and Sheldon were so interested in their book that they didn't see Orson come in. "What are you reading?" asked Orson.

"We're reading about Herman Hamster," replied
Booker. "He's a brave explorer who's always
having adventures in jungles and swamps."

"How come we never get to explore neat
places like that?" asked Sheldon.

"We don't have many jungles around here," said
Orson. "But we could camp overnight in the woods."

"Let's go!" cried the two chicks.

Booker and Sheldon decided to ask their friends to come along. Bo thought a camping trip was a wonderful idea. And Lanolin agreed to come, too, although she was certain it would rain.

Wade, of course, was afraid. "Those woods could be full of hungry bears!" he said.

"There's nothing in those woods except squirrels," Orson assured him.

"I'm afraid of squirrels!"

"You should be," said Lanolin, "because you're a nut!"

Finally, they persuaded Wade to join them.

The gang split up to hunt for camping supplies.
They quickly collected a tent, flashlights, air
mattresses, and marshmallows.

As they were about to leave, Roy appeared.
"What's going on here?" he said.

"We're going camping," explained Orson. "Care
to come along?"

"Camp with you turkeys?" said Roy. "No way!"

The other animals sighed with relief. "It's just as well," said Orson, "since you'd probably try to ruin things for the rest of us."

"Now that sounds like fun!" exclaimed Roy. "Count me in!"

"Way to go, Pig Brain," grumbled Lanolin.

The campers hiked into the thick woods.

"Stay together," said Orson. "We don't want anyone to get lost."

"You babies can barely find your way out of the barn," cracked Roy.

Every bush and shadow made Wade shudder. "I'm glad I brought plenty of bear spray," he said.

"It is kind of spooky in here," remarked Bo.

That gave Roy an idea for some scary fun.
"I just hope we don't run into . . . Wolfbear,"
he said.

"Wolfbear?" croaked Wade. "Who's that?"

All the animals stared anxiously at Roy. "I can't
tell you," he whispered. "It's too horrible!"

In a short time they came to a clearing
deep in the woods.

"This looks like a good campsite,"
said Orson.

"I don't know," countered Roy.
"This looks like Wolfbear country to me."

"AAAAAAH!" cried Wade. "Did you hear that, Orson? This is Wolfbear country!"

"Let's go home!" said Booker.

"Don't be silly!" replied Orson. "Roy's just trying to scare us."

"He's doing a good job," stated Sheldon.

It was time to set up camp.

Orson and Lanolin tried to pitch the tent.

"Something tells me this isn't right," said Orson.

"Maybe we should use these tent poles," suggested Lanolin.

Bo and Booker gathered
wood for the fire . . .

. . . while Sheldon and Wade
inflated the air mattresses.

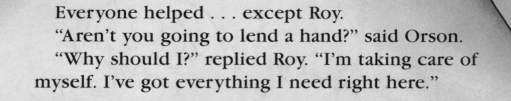

Everyone helped . . . except Roy.
"Aren't you going to lend a hand?" said Orson.
"Why should I?" replied Roy. "I'm taking care of myself. I've got everything I need right here."

After everyone had eaten dinner and all the plates had been cleaned and stacked, the gang sat around the campfire, toasting marshmallows.

"Isn't this fun?" said Orson.

"Herman Hamster couldn't do better than this!" chirped Booker.

That evening, it grew very quiet in the woods. The campfire popped and crackled. An owl hooted.

Suddenly the campers heard a bloodcurdling screech!

"What was that?" cried Lanolin.

"Sorry," said Wade. "I sat on a pine cone."

Just then Roy loomed in the firelight. "Well, well," he said. "If it isn't Wolfbear's favorite snack."

"Marshmallows?" said Bo.

"Campers," said Roy.

All the animals except Orson begged Roy to tell them more about Wolfbear.

"All right," agreed Roy. "If you think you can
handle it."

He began speaking in a low, scary voice.

"Wolfbear is the most cunning, most terrifying,
most awesome monster the world has ever seen.
He has the head of a wolf, with yellow eyes and
long, razor-sharp fangs dripping with blood.

"He stands twelve feet tall, with the body of a bear and claws like knives that can slice the feathers right off a duck." At this, Wade fainted. "And when there's a full moon, like tonight, Wolfbear slinks through the forest until he spies a campfire. Slowly and secretly he stalks the unsuspecting campers. And then . . .

. . . HE STRIKES!"

"AAAAAAH!" shrieked the whole gang.

"And now it's time for bed," said Roy. "Pleasant dreams."

"Suddenly I don't feel very sleepy," said Sheldon.

But Roy had no intention of going to bed.
I'll slip into the woods and sneak up behind
their tent, thought Roy. Then I'll make some
horrible growling noises that will have those
turkeys racing back to the barnyard!

But it was very dark in the woods. The trees were so thick that Roy soon lost sight of the campfire. He stumbled over rocks. Branches clawed at him. He was certain that the campsite was just beyond the next bush, but all he found there was more woods!

Don't panic, Roy said to himself. I mean, why panic? Because I'm lost in deep, dark woods full of huge, ferocious beasts, that's why!

Then Roy heard a rustling noise in the bushes.
"What's that?" he said, his whole body
trembling. "Who's there? Could it be Wolfbear?
That's silly—it couldn't be. I just made him up,
didn't I?"

Suddenly he saw a pair of big yellow eyes!
"AAAAAAH! It's Wolfbear!" cried Roy. "Orson!
Booker! Help! Save me!"

Back at camp, the other animals were all too frightened to sleep.

"What's that awful racket?" asked Sheldon.

"That sounds like Roy," replied Orson. "I think he's in trouble!"

"Poor Roy!" cried Bo. "I bet Wolfbear's got him!"

"We've got to do something!" said Orson.

"But Wolfbear will make camper sandwiches
out of us!" argued Lanolin.

"If we all stick together, maybe we can help
him," said Orson. "Come on!"

Wade moaned. "I wish I'd brought a bigger can
of bear spray!"

Orson and Booker grabbed flashlights and
dashed into the woods, with the other animals
right behind them. Roy was still screaming loudly,
and they followed the sound of his voice. In a
short time they found Roy clinging to a branch,
so frightened that the whole tree was shaking!
"Look out!" he shouted. "It's Wolfbear!"

Booker shined his flashlight where Roy was
pointing.

"AAAAAAH! It's horrible!" shrieked Wade.

"It's a baby raccoon," said Booker.
Roy stopped screaming. He stared at the baby
raccoon. "I knew that," he said with an
embarrassed grin.

Later, Roy made popcorn for everyone.

"I guess sticking together is important," said Roy.

"Were you really scared?" asked Booker.

"Me? Scared? I'm not scared of ANYTHING!" insisted Roy. Then he whispered to Wade, "Would you mind if I borrowed your bear spray?"